W9-CNF-937

# COTTONTAIL RABBITS

by Kristin Ellerbusch Gallagher

Pull Ahead Books

Lerner Publications Company • Minneapolis

*This book is available in two editions:*
Library binding by Lerner Publications Company
Soft cover by First Avenue Editions
Divisions of Lerner Publishing Group
241 First Avenue North, Minneapolis, MN 55401 U.S.A.

Website address: www.lernerbooks.com

Words in *italic type* are explained in a glossary
on page 30.

Library of Congress Cataloging-in-Publication Data

Gallagher, Kristin Ellerbusch.
    Cottontail rabbits / by Kristin Ellerbusch Gallagher.
        p. cm. — (Pull ahead books)
    Includes index.
    Summary: Describes the physical characteristics,
behavior, and habitat of the North American cottontail
rabbit.
    ISBN 0-8225-3617-X (hc : alk. paper)
    ISBN 0-8225-3623-4 (pbk. : alk. paper)
    1. Cottontails—Juvenile literature. [1. Cottontails.
2. Rabbits.] I. Title. II. Series.
QL737.L32G35  2001
599.32'4—dc21                           98-31771

Manufactured in the United States of America
1 2 3 4 5 6 — JR — 06 05 04 03 02 01

Do you see something hiding
in the grass?

What do you think it is?

This animal is a cottontail rabbit.

The cottontail rabbit is named for its tail. The tail looks like a cotton ball.

What a soft place to sit!

Cottontail rabbits have long ears and strong legs.

Short front legs help them balance.

Long back legs help them hop,
the way you might play leapfrog.

Cottontail rabbits have furry paws.

There are claws on each paw.
Claws are like fingernails or toenails.

THUMP! A cottontail stomps
its back foot.

What do you think
thumping means?

# Thumping means DANGER!

Cottontails thump when a *predator* like this fox comes near.

Predators are animals that
eat other animals.

When predators come,
cottontails hide.

A grown cottontail lives in a hole called a *form.* The form is hidden.

How
did this
cottontail
hide its
form?

A mother cottontail makes a nest
when she is ready to have babies.

First she digs a little hole and puts
leaves and grass in it.

Then she pulls fur from her belly to make the nest soft.

A mother cottontail is called a *doe*. Her babies are called *kits*.

Newborn rabbits have no fur.
They cannot see or hear.

A newborn rabbit is so small,
it could fit into a teaspoon.

How big were you when
you were born?

The doe *nurses* her kits.

When she nurses the kits,
she feeds them milk from her body.

Soon the kits grow fur.
Soon they can see and hear.

Kits nurse for about five weeks.
While they nurse, they grow teeth.

Cottontails
use their
teeth to eat
plants.

Cottontails also use their teeth to pick dirt out of their fur.

They *groom* their fur to keep it clean and neat.

A cottontail uses its furry paws
like a washcloth.

First it licks its paws.

Then it wipes each ear clean
with a wet paw.

Cottontails groom their fur
many times a day.

How many times a day
do you wash up?

Cottontail rabbits live in many kinds of places.

Cottontail rabbits live in
the city and the country.

They may even live in
your backyard!

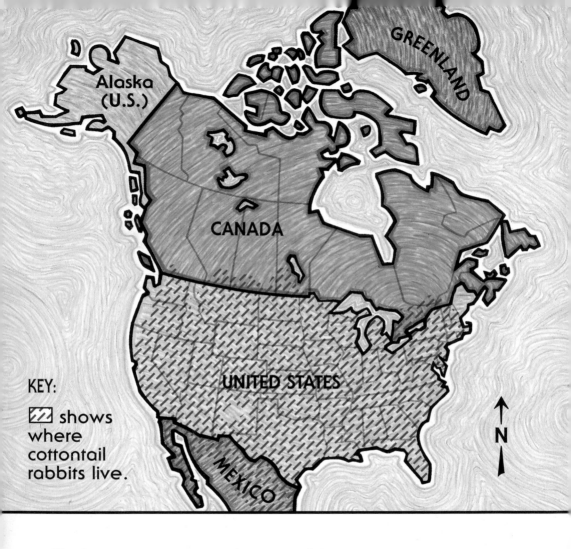

KEY:

⬛ shows where cottontail rabbits live.

Find your state or province on this map.
Do cottontail rabbits live near you?

# Parts of a Cottontail Rabbit's Body

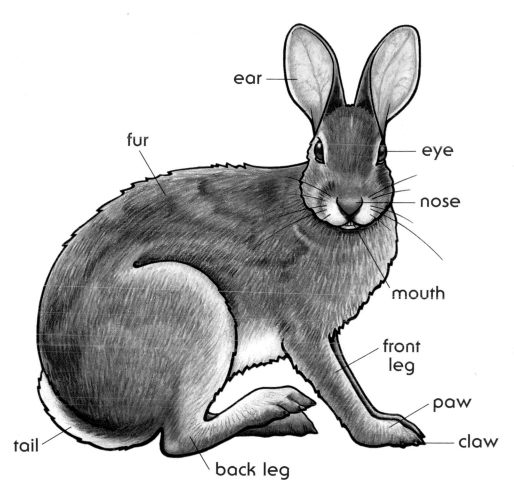

ear

fur

eye

nose

mouth

front
leg

paw

claw

tail

back leg

29

# Glossary

**doe:** a mother cottontail rabbit

**form:** a hole where cottontail rabbits live

**groom:** to keep fur clean and neat

**kits:** baby cottontail rabbits

**nurses:** feeds babies milk from the mother's body

**predator:** an animal that eats other animals

# Hunt and Find

- **baby** cottontails on pages 15–19, 31
- a cottontail **eating** on pages 20, 25, 27
- a cottontail **grooming** its fur on pages 21–24
- a cottontail **hopping** on page 7
- a doe **nursing** kits on page 18

The publisher wishes to extend special thanks to our **series consultant,** Sharyn Fenwick. An elementary science-math specialist, Mrs. Fenwick was the recipient of the National Science Teachers Association 1991 Distinguished Teaching Award. In 1992, representing the state of Minnesota at the elementary level, she received the Presidential Award for Excellence in Math and Science Teaching.

# About the Author

Kristin Ellerbusch Gallagher began writing when she was a kid. She would write letters to an aunt who lived in a nursing home. Kristin loved to write her aunt, because she could feel her listening. Kristin lives with her husband and their dog in Minnesota.

# Photo Acknowledgments

The photographs in this book are reproduced through the courtesy of: © Joe McDonald, cover, p. 25 (top); © Michael H. Francis, back cover, p. 25 (bottom); © Norvia Behling, p. 3; © Leonard Lee Rue III, pp. 4, 7, 12, 13, 14, 22, 23, 24; © Em Ahart, pp. 5, 8; © Tom J. Ulrich, p. 6; © Justin W. Moore, p. 9; © Rich Kirchner, pp. 10, 31; © Jerry Hennen, pp. 11, 17; © E. R. Degginger/Bruce Coleman, Inc., p. 15; © Lynda Richardson/Corbis, pp. 16, 18; © Gay Bumgarner/Tony Stone Images, p. 19; © Len Rue Jr., p. 20; © Tom Vezo/Peter Arnold, Inc., p. 21; © Wendy Shattil/Bob Rozinski, p. 26; © Henry F. Zeman, p. 27.